OLD RED'S
Christmas

Printed in the United States of America
First Printing, 2021
ISBN 979-8-9850580-0-0

Edited by Jen Payne, Words by Jen (Branford, CT)

PUBLISHING

Sterling, Connecticut
www.artistmarnie.com

Dedicated To...

those who love a pretty red tractor!

And to you, the reader,
who enjoys my books.

Thank You!

Old Red enjoyed her days spent with
her new family. Life was good.

One day, the man from the Christmas
tree farm came to visit Old Red.
His green tractor had broken down
and he wanted to borrow her for the
upcoming holiday season.

Old Red's owner knew the man well, and agreed to let her help at the Christmas tree farm.

Red's owner polished her so she shined brightly, making her owner proud.

The next day, Red drove to the Christmas tree farm. She was excited for her new adventure!

Red waited patiently while her owner and the tree farmer talked. She felt so pretty against the bright snow!

Red's owner parked her in the barn,
and his friend gave him a ride home.
Red was excited, knowing she would be
very useful in the days ahead.

The next day was a busy one! Red was up bright and early helping to get the tree farm ready for customers. She towed the bailer out to its spot where it would wrap the trees for customers.

She brought the farmer all over
his farm, where he made last minute
trims to trees and made sure the farm
was ready for visitors!

At the end of the hectic day, Red
was filled up with fuel so she would
be ready for the busy days ahead!

The next day was Saturday and lots of
people arrived to visit the farm and
purchase trees. Old Red felt very festive
with a wreath hung on her grill.

Red enjoyed seeing the smiles on the visitors' faces as she drove past them, the snow crunching noisily under her tires. Her engine was a steady rhythm, the sound of it breaking the silent winter day, and alerting the visitors that she was coming through!

The farmer hooked her to a wagon, and Red happily pulled customers all over the picturesque farm so they could find the perfect tree!

After taking people for rides, the farmer parked her between some decorated trees near the entrance to the fields.

Red proudly posed for photos with visitors. Her wreath and bright red paint against the Christmas trees made a festive display that everyone enjoyed!

The days passed quickly,
and the tree farm
closed for the season.
Red's owner came to
collect her, and they
drove back home where
she belonged. It was
nice to be needed, but
Red was happy to
return to her familiar
barn and beloved
family.

When they got home, Red saw bright lights in her family's window. She drove up close and saw a Christmas tree glowing!

It was a thank you gift to her family
from the Christmas tree farm for all of
her hard work.

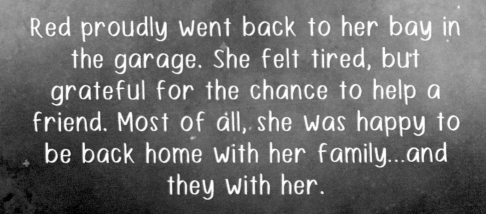

Red proudly went back to her bay in
the garage. She felt tired, but
grateful for the chance to help a
friend. Most of all, she was happy to
be back home with her family...and
they with her.

Merry Christmas to all!
Hope your holiday is filled with love
and happiness!

Thank you for reading my book! When not writing or illustrating, I am painting and dreaming of traveling with my loved ones. I have a website, artistmarnie.com, where you can see more of my colorful, happy work.

Marnie

My other books are:

Discover where your cousins live with a map of the USA and learn about family with somebushy-tailed squirrels and then fill out a family tree together!

A sentimental tale of tending flowers with mom, daughter and then granddaughter. Learn about flowers and how life goes on after empty nest.

Old Red's Adventures... colorful stories about a restored tractor on her farm.

Observe and learn to appreciate the little things, while enjoying illustrations of Beavertail lighthouse in Jamestown, Rhode Island.

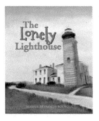

Enjoy the story of an antique car, and learn about combustion engines and the differences between modern cars and a Model A!

Learn why animals may be near the road, and instill a compassion in your children for wildlife.

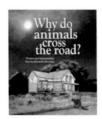

Read all about how much aunties love their family, and how to show you love them in return.

A tale about making bath time fun and stimulating children's imagination.

Observe a kitty growing up in a shelter, and learn how shelters help animals in need! 100% of profits from book go to Paws Cat Shelter, in Woodstock, CT.

Made in the USA
Monee, IL
14 November 2024

70134455R00021